PUCKSTER'S FIRST HOCKEY GAME

CANADA

FENN
TUNDRA

PUCKSTER

BY LORNA SCHULTZ NICHOLSON
ILLUSTRATED BY KELLY FINDLEY

The referee raised his hand and blew a long blast from his whistle. It was time to start the game! Puckster could hardly believe the big day was finally here. He and his friends had been practising on the outdoor rink for weeks, but today they were finally playing in a real arena, in a real game, against a real team.

 2

Puckster grinned at his teammates as they took their positions. Roly was in net. Manny and Sarah were ready on defence. And Puckster centred the forward line between Francois and Charlie. At the other end of the rink, the Raccoon Rockets were getting ready too.

Puckster held his breath as the referee dropped the puck. The game was on!

Puckster won the faceoff and attempted a pass to Francois. Francois was a big player for his age. He was strong and could barrel by most everyone. But the puck slid past Francois and landed right on the stick of a Rockets player. Luckily, Manny the Moose was a sharp defender. He spun his sled around to stop the speedy Rockets player in his tracks.

"You can't get by me!" he yelled.

And he was right. He poked the puck free and Sarah skated quickly toward it. Using her perfectly perfected crossovers, she whirled behind the net and then stopped. She looked up the ice to see where everyone was positioned. She needed to set up a scoring play – and fast.

Puckster was blasting up the middle of the ice with Francois beside him on his wing. Sarah saw her chance! She fired the puck to Francois who quickly passed it to Puckster. Puckster looked to pass to Charlie, but Charlie was spinning and twirling across the ice, barely staying on his feet.

"Charlie, get ready!" Puckster yelled to his friend.

But before Puckster could make his pass, a Rockets player snatched the puck.

Puckster quickly changed directions and gave chase, but it was too late.

The Rockets carried the puck down the ice. When their centre crossed the blue line, he wound up for a huge slap shot. The puck sailed under Roly's glove and into the net. Everyone was disappointed – especially Charlie.

"Don't worry!" Sarah yelled, giving her teammate a pat on the back as she skated past. "We'll get it back!"

Puckster smiled as he stepped into the faceoff circle again. This was even better than he'd thought it would be. His friends were beside him, the crowd was cheering, and he was playing real live hockey. He didn't even care that they were down by a goal.

Puckster won the faceoff again and passed the puck to Francois. Francois skated hard toward the net and blasted a shot right into the five-hole, between the goalie's pads. The red goal light came on and Puckster and his pals celebrated with high-fives.

But it was a short celebration. On the very next play, the Rockets scored again. "Don't worry!" Sarah yelled as she skated by a dejected Roly. "We can get it back!"

Puckster was determined to tie the game up. He sent the puck back to Sarah. She rushed forward across the blue line and yelled, "Cover me!"

Puckster watched with excitement as Sarah weaved around the Rockets defender and sniped off a shot that sailed into the opposing team's net.

At the end of the first period the score was 2-2. Puckster gathered his team on the bench for a pep talk. "We're doing great!" he said, taking a long drink from his water bottle. Sarah nodded in agreement.

"Phew," Francois panted as he wiped the sweat off his face. "I'm tired."

 10

Roly stood on the ice, stretching to stay limber. The fans cheered at how he could easily touch his toes.

At the far end of the bench, Charlie hung his head. "I haven't touched the puck yet," he said. His voice was small and quiet.

When the referee dropped the puck at the beginning of the next period, Puckster slapped it over to Charlie. He was so excited that the puck got caught in his big tail. Charlie started to spin. He was still spinning like a top when the Rockets stole the puck and scored.

"Don't worry!" Sarah said, laughing. "We can get that one back too!"

On the next play, Francois had the puck. Puckster skated hard toward the net. Sure

enough, Francois found him open. With the puck on the end of his stick and defenders barrelling down the ice, Puckster wondered what he should do. Shoot or deke?

When the Rockets goalie left his crease, Puckster made up his mind. He deked to the left and sent a backhander into the upper corner of the net.

"Wow!" said Sarah, hugging Puckster.

"What an awesome goal!" said Manny.

"I wish I could do that," said Charlie.

13

At the end of the second period the score was 4-4. The Rockets had scored again, but then Manny had tied it up with a big booming blast from the blue line.

"Everyone has scored but me," said Charlie.

"And me!" Roly laughed.

Francois playfully hip-checked Roly. "You don't count," he said, laughing. "You're a goalie."

"But I count," said Charlie, shaking his head. "I just get so nervous out there with the crowd watching."

Sarah patted Charlie on the back. "Forget about the crowd," she said.

"Pretend you're at practice," said Manny.

"Yeah, in practice you always score against me," said Roly.

The buzzer sounded to start the third period and everyone skated back onto the ice.

15

The third period flew by. Not a single goal was scored until, with three minutes left on the game clock, the Rockets put one into the net. Roly collapsed on the ice, covering his face with his big goalie glove.

"It's okay, Roly," said Francois. "That was a really tough shot."

"Even Roberto Luongo couldn't have stopped that," said Puckster.

"You're right," said Roly. He stood up, shrugged his shoulders, and dusted the ice and snow from his pads.

"We can get it back!" Charlie said with his squeaky voice.

On the very next faceoff the puck skidded in Charlie's direction. He took a deep breath as he skated forward, remembering what his teammates had said. He pretended he was at practice. It was easy! There was Roly in the net – just like at the outdoor rink. Charlie smiled and skated as fast as he could toward his friend.

 18

"You're going the wrong way, Charlie!" everyone yelled.

But Charlie was going so fast he didn't know how to stop!

Sarah and Francois froze. Puckster and Manny covered their eyes. For a second or two, no one knew what to do. Then, Puckster had an idea.

"Charlie!" he yelled as loud as he could. "Spin around like Sidney Crosby does!"

So Charlie spun. And he spun and he spun all the way down the ice – right toward the Rockets net.

"Shoot!" the crowd yelled. "Shoot the puck!"

So Charlie smacked at the rolling puck. Everyone watched as it bounced toward the net.

The goalie reached out his glove hand to catch it, but the puck bounced right over his trapper and landed on the goal line. It teetered there for a second before tipping into the net. Just then, the buzzer sounded to end the game.

"It's in!" yelled Sarah. "Charlie did it! He tied the game!"

Later, the team celebrated in the dressing room. Everyone was thrilled with the outcome of their first real game. Charlie was the happiest of all.

"I love hockey," he said, grinning from ear to ear. "But boy do I ever have a lot to learn."

"We all do," said Puckster, laughing. "All the Team Canada players, like Hayley Wickenheiser and Jayna Hefford, were just like us when they were young. They had lots to learn too! But we're a team and we'll learn together. That's what makes hockey so much fun!"

PUCKSTER

PUCKSTER'S HOCKEY TIP:

A **deke** is when a player fakes a forehand shot, pulls the puck to the backhand, and shoots either high or low. It can also be when a player pulls the puck to the backhand, fakes a shot, brings the puck quickly to the forehand, and shoots into the open net.

Good luck!

PUCKSTER'S TIPS:

1. Every person on a team is important.

2. Always encourage your teammates by saying positive words.

3. Never give up and always play your hardest.